Parent's Introduction

Whether your child is a beginning reader, a reluctant reader, or an eager reader, this book offers a fun and easy way to encourage and help your child in reading.

Developed with reading education specialists, *We Both Read* books invite you and your child to take turns reading aloud. You read the left-hand pages of the book, and your child reads the right-hand pages—which have been written at one of six early reading levels. The result is a wonderful new reading experience and faster reading development!

You may find it helpful to read the entire book aloud yourself the first time, then invite your child to participate the second time. As you read, try to make the story come alive by reading with expression. This will help to model good fluency. It will also be helpful to stop at various points to discuss what you are reading. This will help increase your child's understanding of what is being read.

In some books, a few challenging words are introduced in the parent's text, distinguished with **bold** lettering. Pointing out and discussing these words can help to build your child's reading vocabulary. If your child is a beginning reader, it may be helpful to run a finger under the text as each of you reads. Please also notice that a "talking parent" ⌒ icon precedes the parent's text, and a "talking child" ⌒ icon precedes the child's text.

If your child struggles with a word, you can encourage "sounding it out," but keep in mind that not all words can be sounded out. Your child might pick up clues about a word from the picture, other words in the sentence, or any rhyming patterns. If your child struggles with a word for more than five seconds, it is usually best to simply say the word.

Most of all, remember to praise your child's efforts and keep the reading fun. After you have finished the book, ask a few questions and discuss what you have read together. Rereading this book multiple times may also be helpful for your child.

Try to keep the tips above in mind as you read together, but don't worry about doing everything right. Simply sharing the enjoyment of reading together will increase your child's reading skills and help to start your child off on a lifetime of reading enjoyment!

Kecko the Gecko

A We Both Read Book: Level 1
Guided Reading: Level F

_____

Text Copyright © 2018 by Sindy McKay
Illustrations Copyright © 2018 by Meredith Johnson
All rights reserved

We Both Read® is a trademark of Treasure Bay, Inc.

Published by
Treasure Bay, Inc.
P. O. Box 119
Novato, CA 94948 USA

Printed in Malaysia

Library of Congress Control Number: 2017946612

ISBN: 978-1-60115-304-3

Visit us online at:
TreasureBayBooks.com

PR-10-17

Kecko the Gecko

By Sindy McKay

with illustrations by Meredith Johnson

Kecko looked up at Matt with his big sad gecko eyes.

"I'm sorry," said Matt. "Today is the first day of school, and I have to **leave** you here. Alone."

Matt felt bad. He did not want to **leave Kecko**.

3

 Kecko was a crested gecko lizard and was the best birthday gift Matt had ever received. Matt had taken care of Kecko all summer.

He made sure Kecko's home was warm and clean.

4

Matt fed him and kept him safe.
He spent lots of time with him.

Now it was the start of a new **school** year and Matt was afraid that Kecko would be lonely while he was away.

Then Matt had an idea. "Kecko doesn't have to stay home," he thought.

"Kecko can go to **school**, too!
I will hide him! No one will see
him!"

When Matt arrived at school, his friend Kim asked if he was sad about leaving Kecko at home. Matt grinned and unzipped his **backpack**. Kecko poked his head out and Kim squealed.

"Kecko!" She took him from the **backpack**. "You are so cute!"

The bell rang and Matt quickly tucked Kecko into his shirt and got in line. Everyone streamed into the classroom.

At his desk, Matt felt Kecko's claws tickle him under his collar.

The girl next to Matt saw Kecko
on his neck.
"EEK!!"

As Mrs. Jackson rushed over to see what happened, Matt whispered, "Please don't tell, Anna!"

"Sorry, Mrs. Jackson," said Anna. "I, uh, thought my backpack was **gone**, but it's not."

Matt gave Anna a grateful smile.

But where was Kecko?? He was not in his shirt. Kecko was **gone**!

Kim leaned forward in her desk and whispered,
"There he is! By the pencil sharpener!"

She rose quickly from her desk. "I'll go sharpen my
pencil and **try** to **catch** him."

Kim snuck up on Kecko. She
did **try** to **catch** him.

Kecko scurried away so fast that Kim was only able to catch his **tail**. When the **tail** broke off in her hand, she slapped her hand across her mouth to keep from shrieking!

Kecko ran off. His **tail** was still in Kim's hand!

Kim rushed back and told Matt what had happened. "It's okay," he assured her. "A gecko's tail is designed to break off so he can get away from predators."

18

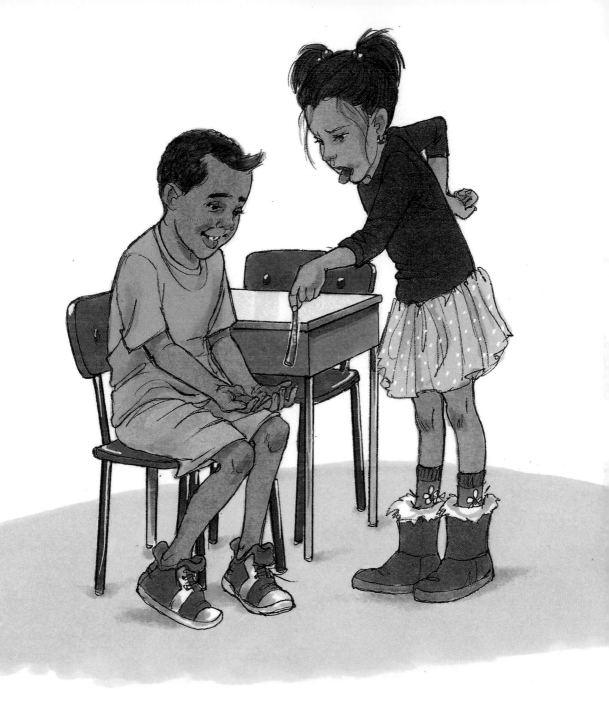

Kim gave the tail to Matt. She was glad to get rid of it!

Just then Tom turned around to Matt and pointed up.
"Hey! There's a lizard on the wall! **Cool**!"

Matt raced over to get him, but Kecko scurried up the
wall and ran across the ceiling.

"That is so **cool**!" said Tom.

"How can he do that**??**"

Before Matt could answer, **Mrs. Jackson** called out to him. "Matt Williams! Why are you jumping on your desk? Please get down right now!"

"Oh! Um, I'm just jumping because, um, . . . because I'm so excited about being back at school!" replied Matt.

 "Well, sit down," said **Mrs. Jackson**.

Matt sat down.

Mrs. Jackson headed for the bookcase.

"Oh no," whispered Kim. "Look! Kecko jumped down on top of the bookcase. Now Mrs. Jackson is going to see him for sure!"

Kecko made a big jump. Mrs. Jackson did not see him land.

Matt and his friends watched in horror as Mrs. Jackson walked back to her desk with Kecko nestled in her hair. The other students began to giggle as Kecko lifted his head and looked around.

Kim put her hand up. Mrs. Jackson came to her desk.

While Kim asked Mrs. Jackson a question about multi-plication, Matt reached over to try and snatch Kecko off her **head**. Only Kecko did not want to be snatched. He liked it there!

Mrs. Jackson went back to her desk. Kecko jumped off her **head**.

He landed on the back of her **chair**. Now everyone in class was laughing loudly. Mrs. Jackson rose from her **seat** and demanded to know, "What is so funny?"

Kecko jumped down to land
on the **seat** of her **chair**.

Mrs. Jackson looked sternly at her students, waiting for an answer. Everyone stopped laughing.

She started to sit back down again and Matt saw that she was about to sit right on top of poor Kecko!

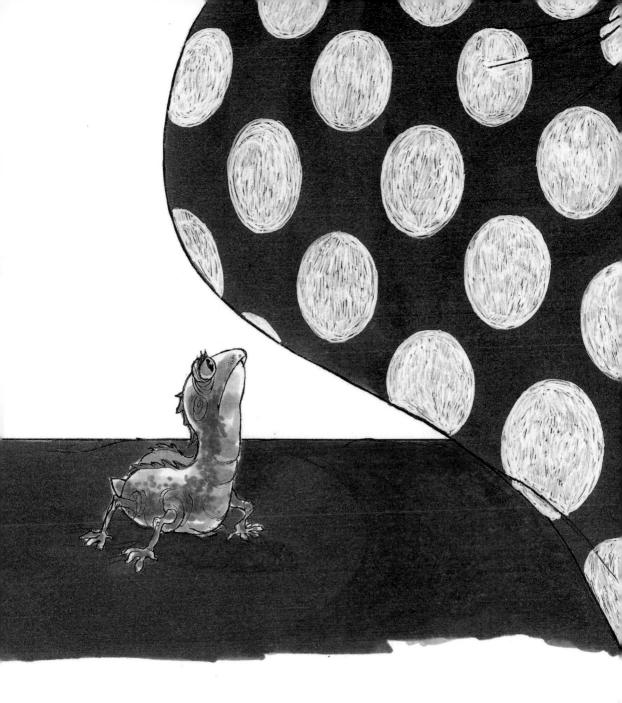

Matt yelled out, "Mrs. Jackson! Do not sit on Kecko!"

Mrs. Jackson stopped just in time. She looked down at the seat behind her and saw Kecko looking up at her with his big eyes.

"Okay," she said. "Who brought a **gecko** to school?"

 Matt did not want to put his hand up, but he had to. Kecko was his **gecko**.

Mrs. Jackson **told** Matt that it was not okay to bring a
pet to school without asking. He must never do it again!

"But since he's here now, why don't you tell us what
you know about geckos."

Matt **told** the class how to set up a gecko's home.

He told them that crested geckos eat bugs and fruit and that they have adhesive toe pads that allow them to walk up walls and across ceilings.

Matt held up Kecko's tail and told them how it came off.

Mrs. Jackson thanked Matt and told him that Kecko was
welcome to visit the class again, but they should discuss
it ahead of time so a safe space could be prepared for
Kecko. "Do you **think** he would like to visit us again some-
day?" she asked.

"Yes," Matt said. "Kecko will
be back. I **think** he likes it here!"

If you liked **Kecko the Gecko**, here are some other
We Both Read® books you are sure to enjoy!

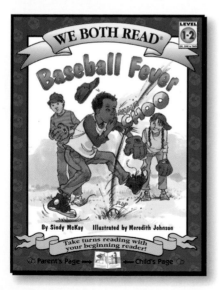

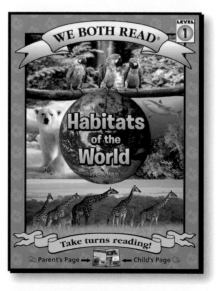

To see all the We Both Read books that are available,
just go online to **WeBothRead.com**